D1238950

A QUIET PLACE

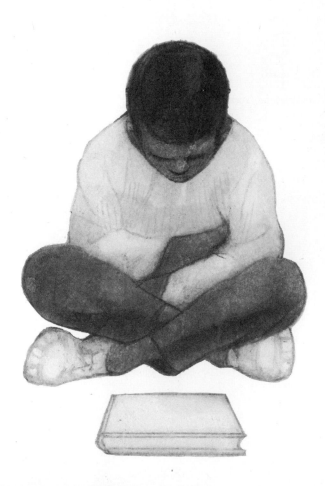

A QUIET PLACE

By ROSE BLUE

Pictures by Tom Feelings

Franklin Watts, Inc.
575 Lexington Avenue
New York, N.Y. 10022

To Frieda and Irving

Copyright © 1969 by Rose Bluestone
Library of Congress Catalog Card Number: 69-11223
Printed in the United States of America

A QUIET PLACE

Matthew stared straight ahead and read the sign over and over again. He closed his eyes but in his mind he could still see the sign that hung on the wall over the librarian's desk: "LIBRARY CLOSES AUGUST 25. RETURN BOOKS TO BOOKMOBILE LIBRARY."

Matthew opened his eyes and gazed out the window, across the patch of green grass on the tiny library lawn, to the other sign on the sidewalk. He could not see the printing but he knew the words by heart: "UNDER CONSTRUCTION — THE NEW MADISON LIBRARY. TO OPEN IN EIGHTEEN MONTHS TO TWO YEARS."

Two years. Matthew tried to picture two whole years. An autumn, then a winter, then a spring, then another summer. Then autumn, winter, spring, and summer all over again. It was too hard to imagine such a faraway time. When you are nine and a half, two years seems like forever. Tomorrow Matthew would come to the library for the very last time. He would walk up the stone steps, through the side door, then up another flight to the children's room. He would go way back past the biographies, to where hardly anyone ever came, and sink into his yellow chair that squished down like a pillow when he sat on it.

Tomorrow it would all be over. Matthew was losing his quiet place. No more could he come here when his baby brother cried and his big sister played her radio real loud and the noise in the house got to be too much. No more could he come here and read his books. No more could he stare out the window, and think and dream and remember.

Now Matthew looked out at the hazy August sky and thought back to the first place he could remember. He had been very little, and he had lived in a children's shelter, where he shared a cottage with eleven other boys. Sometimes boys would leave the cottage to go home or to live with other families. And sometimes new boys would come and they would be sad and lonesome and cry for a long time because they missed their homes. But Matthew didn't remember any home, and when he asked the big people at the shelter if he had once had a real mommy and daddy like some of the new boys, they turned away or talked about other things, like grown-ups do when they don't know the answer or don't want to tell. So Matthew never really knew. But lots of times he would wonder.

When Matthew was six he went to live with the Reardon family and became a foster child. The Reardons yelled a lot. Mr. Reardon would

come home late and make noise and Mrs. Reardon would yell at him. They both yelled at Matthew and sometimes hit him — he didn't know why. Then one day the welfare lady came and Mrs. Reardon said, "The money don't but cover what it takes to feed and dress him. If that's all you people give it hardly pays to keep him."

Next day the welfare people came and took Matthew from the Reardons and he went to live with a family named Grant. Mr. Grant hardly ever came home. Mrs. Grant didn't yell so much, but she was very grouchy. Once, when Matthew called her "Mama," she got very mad and said, "I'm not your mama. Call me Mrs. Grant." And Matthew felt sad deep through and wished he were back at the shelter where he had other boys around him and people were kinder.

It was strange, but when Matthew thought back, the Grants and the Reardons got all jumbled up together in his mind and he tried to remember and forget all at the same time. The time at the shelter seemed clearer even though it had happened so long ago.

Then a year and two months ago, at the start of last summer, the welfare people came again.

12

They told Matthew he would go to live with another family whose two sons were all grown-up and in the Army. The family had already taken in a baby boy, but they wanted still more children because they were lonesome and missed their boys. So now Matthew would have another foster-mother — her name was Mrs. Walters.

The apartment the Walters family lived in seemed comfortable and clean and Mrs. Walters was kind-looking, and a little bit fat, the way Matthew felt a real mother should be. When the welfare lady said, "Matthew, this is your new foster-mother," he said, "Hello, Mrs. Walters," polite as could be.

Mrs. Walters put her arms around Matthew and cuddled him. She said in a gentle, but sure way, "Mrs. Walters? Now you listen here, sugar, I'm your *mama* from now on, and that's what you call me."

Mama's arms felt warm, and Matthew was home for the first time since he had left the shelter.

A few days later the welfare lady came back again, and Matthew heard her say, "She's a handful."

Mama said, "That's okay. I always wanted a daughter."

Baby brother Stevie was moved into Matthew's room and a new big sister came to live with them. She was fourteen and very beautiful, a coffee-with-cream color, and her name was Claudia. She was kind to Matthew and soon he got to love her a lot.

So Matthew had a mama and a papa and a big sister and a baby brother, and now it seemed as if before had never happened, as if his home had always been with the Walters family. But sometimes Matthew would think back and remember other times.

Matthew jumped as a light went off. They were getting ready to close the library for the day. Matthew looked down at the book open on his lap. It was about a boy who lived a long time ago in the West. There were seventy pages and Matthew was up to page 57. He had read only a few pages today. He would come to the library early tomorrow and finish the book. It was too hard to read in his room with Baby Stevie there. Another light went out and Matthew thought of home, where the kitchen was so bright and cozy. It was almost suppertime. Matthew got up and pulled his white T-shirt down over his jeans. He tucked the book under his arm and left the library, walking briskly through the noisy, crowded streets — past the brownstones and tenements, past the people sitting on the stoops, past the overflowing garbage cans, across the avenue, and down the city block.

"Hey, who's that struttin' down the street?" somebody was singing in a teasing voice. Matthew looked and saw the big kid they called Duke standing by the boarded-up house near the corner. In a minute, Duke and a whole bunch of kids were standing around Matthew, clapping and singing.

"Matthew's struttin' down the street," another boy sang in the same beat.

"Struttin', struttin', with his book," Duke chimed in.

"Hey you, what you gonna do with the book?" one of the group asked.

"He's gonna look at the book," Duke sang, and they all laughed.

Matthew swallowed hard and wished Claudia and her friends were there. They were lots bigger than these kids. "Hey, you guys, get lost," Matthew said, trying to sound as tough as he could.

But now all of Duke's friends were standing around Matthew, clapping and singing, like little kids playing circle games in school.

Matthew did a quick hop-skip and ducked under a big kid's arm and out of the circle. He kept walking as fast as he could, trying to look cool, and went up his front stoop two steps at a time, whistling so the big kids wouldn't think he was scared. When the front door closed behind him he held his book tight and walked slowly up two flights of the five-story house to home.

A delicious smell of something cooking led Matthew into the kitchen where Mama was standing at the stove, stirring a great big pot of stew.

Mama turned, said "Hello, Matthew, honey," and kept stirring without losing the rhythm.

"Hello, Mama," Matthew said quietly. He

leaned against the refrigerator awhile, not saying a word.

Mama watched him closely for a long minute. "Anything wrong, Matthew?" she asked.

He shook his head.

"Where you been all day?"

"At the library, Mama," Matthew said softly. "It's closing tomorrow."

Mama stopped stirring. "So that's it," she said, kind of to herself. Then, a little bit louder, she said, "Come over here, sugar."

Matthew walked slowly to the stove and Mama bent down and gave him a great big warm hug. Matthew buried his face against Mama's flowered apron.

"Now," Mama said, "it's not the end of the world. The ladies at the market told me we're getting a library on wheels — a big truck rolling in two times a week. And when the work is all done the new library will be real fine."

Mama took one arm from around Matthew, filled the big wooden stirring spoon with stew, and held it to his mouth. "You take a big taste — it'll warm your tummy."

Matthew swallowed the meat and crisp onions and carrots all mixed together and they went down smooth and warm. He started to feel a little bit better right away.

Footsteps sounded outside the kitchen. When Matthew looked up, Papa was standing there in his blue uniform. Papa was big and strong-looking. He was good to Matthew, but he was tired a lot of the time because he worked so hard delivering people's mail all day.

Papa put his arm around Matthew's shoulder. "Hello, son," he said. "You been a good boy?"

"Yes, Papa," Matthew answered, nodding.

Papa turned to Mama. "Supper ready soon, honey?" he asked.

"Pretty soon now, Papa. Stew has to cook just a little more."

"I'm beat," he said. "Think I'll stretch out awhile. Call me when supper is ready."

"Sure, Papa. You rest yourself. I'll call you."

Mama most always said the same thing when Papa lay down before supper. But when she was cooking something that would keep, she would let Papa sleep, and when he woke up she would warm it up and fill another little dish for herself to keep him company. She and Papa would sit and eat late at night, all by themselves.

Matthew sat down at the kitchen table on the chair nearest the window so he could look out on the street if he felt like it. Claudia bounced in right after Papa lay down, looking prettier than any girl Matthew had ever seen, in her bright summer dress with lots of different colors in it. She leaned down, rumpled Matthew's black curly hair, and said, "How's my little brother doing today?" Then she called, "Mama, I'm home."

Mama said, "I can see that. Where you been all day, girl?"

Claudia shrugged. "Just hanging around with the kids."

Mama said, "Seems to me you could find some time to help your mama," but she didn't act real mad.

"I'll set the table, Mama," Claudia said.

"You do that, sweetie, but don't set a place for Papa. I'll just let him sleep and I'll heat up the stew when he wakes up."

"Mama, is it okay if Roy comes over for supper?"

"Why sure, honey. Now you know you don't have to ask that. We always make do for one more, and Roy is always welcome in this house. He's a good boy."

Roy was Claudia's very best boyfriend, and Matthew liked him better than any other boy Claudia knew. He was Mama's favorite, too — she liked his ideas. Roy was finishing up high school and also working part time. He talked about going on to college, but he was poor and had no daddy, so that meant he would have to work during the day and go to school at night.

Matthew looked out the window and remembered back to last year, when Frankie had been Claudia's boyfriend. Frankie was big and mean-looking and sounded mad at everybody when he talked. He didn't like having Matthew around,

and Claudia would act nasty and get rid of Matthew when Frankie came to see her.

Frankie didn't go to school anymore; just hung around all the time. Mama didn't like him, not one little bit. But Claudia would toss her head and go out with him every night anyway — till the night the policeman brought her home in his car.

Matthew remembered hearing voices and jumping up from his sleep and running to the living room. The policeman was saying, "This time nothing really bad happened, but a girl's folks have to keep an eye on her before she gets into serious trouble." Claudia looked down at the floor and Mama started to cry. Matthew ran to his room, shut the door, and lay down in bed with the covers pulled up around his head as the voices got louder and louder.

When Matthew thought of that night he felt shivery inside all over again, but after that, Frankie never came around anymore, not one more time. Soon Roy got to be Claudia's best boyfriend. Roy liked Matthew a lot and in a while Claudia was acting nice to her brother all the time — even when her boyfriend was there.

Now Matthew looked away from the window as the baby started to cry. Claudia went to get him and led him into the kitchen — Stevie could walk if you held him by one hand. She held him on her lap and said, "I'll give Stevie his bottle, Mama."

Mama said, "Okay, sweetie," and took over setting the table.

When the baby finished his bottle, Claudia put him in his playpen. Then Roy came in. They all sat down and ate supper and talked about lots of things, but quietly, so they wouldn't wake up Papa. After supper, Claudia put Baby Stevie to bed, and Roy and Matthew helped Mama with the dishes. Then Claudia took Roy's hand and said, "Let's go down awhile. It's real pretty out tonight." She held her other hand out to Matthew and said, "You come too."

Sometimes Claudia took Matthew with her and sometimes she didn't, but whenever she did, it always made Matthew feel good. He smiled and asked, "Okay, Mama?"

Mama said, "Okay, but don't stay out too late." Matthew went down with Roy and Claudia, past all the people on the front stoop, and down the block to the corner where Claudia and the big kids on the block hung out.

The big kids stood together — some in twos, some in threes, and some in groups — and Matthew stood with Roy and Claudia, who were leaning against a car.

"This crummy street looks a little better at night," Claudia said.

Matthew looked around. The street did look softer in the foggy night. The darkness dimmed the paper and cans in the street and hid the dingy, no-color of the houses.

"In my library books I see pictures of clean streets with pretty houses and lots of trees," Matthew said. "I wonder where those places are."

"They're not so far away, honey, not so far at all," Claudia said. "But they may as well be on the moon. Fat chance we've got of ever living there. When you're black you can forget it. You can't make it no matter what you do."

"Now, that's enough of that talk, Claudia,"
Roy said, acting stern, the way Papa did at times.

"You're the livin' end, always hitting the
books," Claudia said.

She took Matthew's chin in her hand and
tilted it. "You and my little brother."

"Now, don't you tease your brother," Roy
said. "He's got to go his own way."

"I'll be hitting the books soon, myself,"
Claudia said, "if I go back to school."

"What do you mean *if*, baby?" Roy said.

Claudia shrugged. "I don't know," she said
dreamily. "I've been thinking maybe I'll drop
out and get a job and buy some real groovy
clothes."

"You'll do no such thing, girl," Roy said, getting madder and madder now. "You quit school and your folks will give you what for, and so will I."

"I guess with my folks and you two bugging me, I don't stand a chance. I'll be making the scene at school come September."

"You better believe it," Roy said.

Claudia took her little transistor radio out of her purse, switched it on, and put it on the fender of the car. She started dancing to rock and roll music and put her hand out to Roy, but he was

still mad and wouldn't move away from the car. She turned to Matthew, and he did some dance steps with his sister, and Roy laughed and stopped being mad. Roy came over, and Matthew clapped as Roy and Claudia danced to the music, real smooth, and pretty to watch. They danced until Mama stuck her head out the window and called.

"Matthew, you get right up here now. It's late. And you better be getting up soon too, Claudia."

Matthew's eyes were starting to feel heavy, and he thought of his pillow, but he asked, "Oh, Mama, can't I stay just five more minutes?"

"No," Mama answered a little bit louder. "Now you scoot up here."

Matthew said, "Oh, Mama," but he scooted down the block and up the steps, straight home and to bed.

Matthew promised himself he would get up early, as he did on school days, but next morning Stevie was quiet, and by the time Matthew woke up, Papa had gone to work and Claudia was down with her friends. Mama said, "Sleepyhead, it's near to lunchtime," and she gave him a big meal of hot cereal and bread and jam. After breakfast Matthew got his book and headed for the library. He would be able to finish his book, and after he returned it, there would still be enough time left to think and dream and say good-bye to the children's room and his yellow chair that squished when he sat on it.

As Matthew walked with long steps down the block, Lefty called to him and Matthew turned and waved and said, "Hi, Lefty." Lefty lived four houses down and was in his class at school.

Lefty came up to him and asked, "Where you off to?"

"The library," Matthew said.

"You're a bookworm, man, a real bookworm." Lefty jumped around in front of Matthew, blocking him, and said, "Bookworm,

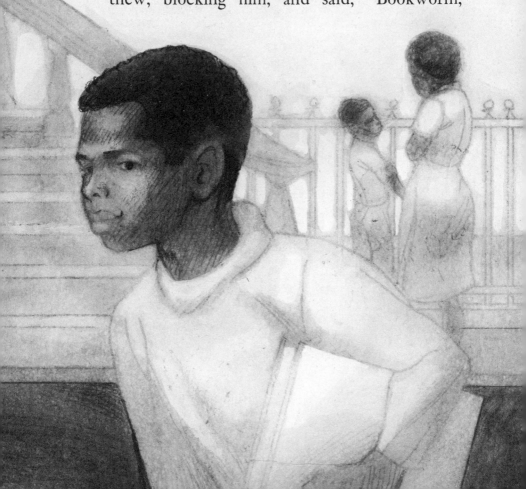

bookworm, bookworm," over and over in a singsong voice.

Matthew said, "Take off, Lefty." He did a little sideways dance step to get out of Lefty's way, and kept going. He didn't want Lefty to think he was running away, so he just took big steps and walked fast.

Lefty had to run to catch up. "Wait up, man, I'll walk you," he said in a friendlier voice.

Matthew and Lefty walked down the block

and across the street, walking slow, then fast; then not stepping on the cracks; then one foot in front of the other, balancing on the edge of the curb. They took a shortcut through an alley, stepping over the broken glass, paper, and cans, and came to a vacant lot where a bunch of boys were tossing a ball back and forth.

"Hey," Lefty said, "we've got enough guys for a game."

Quick as a wink the boys found some wood lying in the lot, and before Matthew knew it he was playing first base in a stickball game. He made some great catches, got three hits, including one triple, and his team won in the last half of the ninth inning. Then Matthew picked up his book from the ground, dusted it off, pulled his T-shirt down, and went on to the library.

He climbed the steps just as he had many, many times before and pushed the front door. But this time the door would not open. Matthew pushed harder and harder but still the door stayed closed. Matthew kept pushing and pushing, even though he knew it was no use, even though he knew it was too late, even though he knew the library was closed. Closed for good.

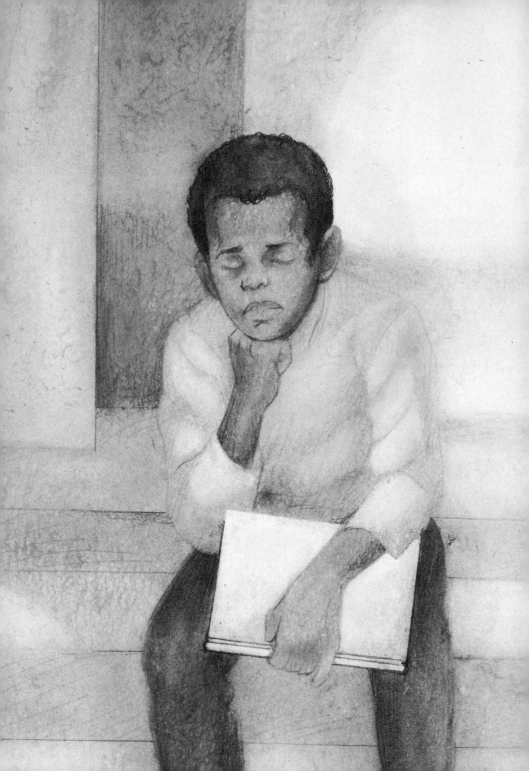

Matthew felt as bad as he had ever felt in his whole life. He sank down onto the stone library steps and just sat there with his chin in his hand. Then he opened the book and read straight through to page 70, to the end, without looking up, without thinking about anything else even for one single second.

He felt glad that things turned out okay for the boy in the old-time West, but as soon as he closed the book he felt sad all over again. He stared out into space. The stone steps felt hard and he thought of the soft yellow chair that he would never see again.

The click-clack of high heels sounded on the stone, and Matthew felt a hand on his arm. He looked up and there stood a pretty lady with long hair. She looked just like Miss Wilson, his teacher last year, and when she spoke her voice sounded sweet and soft, just like Miss Wilson's did.

"We're closed, dear," she said.

Matthew nodded. "I came to bring back my book," he said sadly, "but I came too late."

The lady sat down beside Matthew, right on the steps, as if she didn't even care about dirtying her dress.

"You can return your book tomorrow, you know," she said. "The bookmobile will come every Friday and every Tuesday, and it will be here tomorrow from eleven in the morning till three in the afternoon. It's a real library in a great big truck. Won't that be nice?"

Matthew nodded because he could tell she wanted to cheer him up, but he knew the bookmobile wouldn't be the same. Not the same at all. A truck that came and went away couldn't be like a big brick library that stood in the same place all the time and was there when you needed it.

"You bring back your book," she said, "and I'll help you find a special new one to take out. You come tomorrow. Promise?"

Matthew nodded again. The lady stood up and smiled and then her heels went clicking down the stone steps and up the street. She turned and waved to Matthew. He waved back and sat there a little longer. Then a mean-looking man with a broom came out and said in an angry voice, "Move on, boy." Matthew got up and slowly walked toward home, looking down at the ground all the time. When Matthew got to

his house the blue sadness that he felt deep down was still there and wouldn't go away.

Mama was at the stove. She took one look at Matthew, filled the big wooden spoon to overflowing, and held it out to him. But this time he just took a tiny bit and turned away — even food couldn't help.

"My goodness," Mama said. "First time you didn't gobble up my chicken and dumplings. All my boys always loved that dish."

Matthew leaned against the refrigerator. "Mama," he said in a low voice that was almost a whisper.

"Yes, Matthew," Mama said, still stirring.

"Am I your boy too? Just like your big boys who went away?"

Mama put down her spoon and came to Matthew. "What a silly question," she said, folding him in her arms. "You know you're my boy. Why, when my big boys went to the Army I just moped all the time. Sure, I still worry about them lots, but having a family here to do for just saves me, that's all. And you're my big boy now, Matthew, honey. You're the biggest boy I have at home."

"Are you gonna keep me, Mama?" Matthew asked softly. "Are you gonna be my mama forever and ever?"

"Lord willing, sugar," Mama said, rocking Matthew to her, "Lord willing, forever and ever."

46

Mama drew Matthew closer and hugged him extra tight and extra long. Then the door slammed and Claudia and Roy came into the kitchen, whispering and laughing.

"Set the table, Claudia," Mama said. "Your papa's still sleeping, so he'll eat later."

"Right away, Mama," Claudia said. She put her arm around Matthew and said, "Hello, little brother." But Matthew slipped away from her and walked out of the kitchen toward his room because big boys don't cry, at least not when everyone is looking.

"What's the matter, honey?" Claudia started to walk after him, but Roy held her arm.

"Let him be. Sometimes a boy has to be alone and just make the quiet scene."

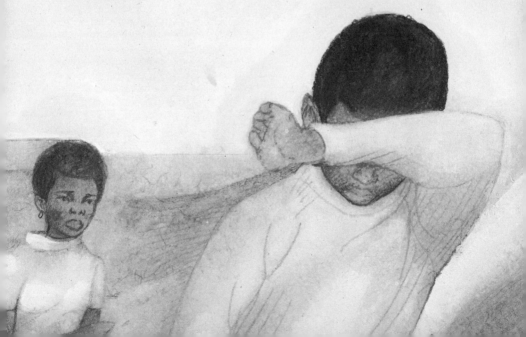

Matthew stayed in his room a long time, lying there staring at the shadows and the cracks in the ceiling, till Baby Stevie woke up and started to cry. Matthew held him and began to feel a little better — holding Stevie made Matthew feel grown-up. When the baby fell asleep again, Matthew put him back in his crib. He was getting pretty hungry, so he left his room and went back into the kitchen.

Mama and Papa were having their late supper the way they did sometimes, sitting and talking grown-up talk, very low, all alone. But tonight Papa said, "Sit here by me, son," and he pulled a chair up to the table.

Mama fixed a big bowl full of steamy hot chicken and dumplings, and Matthew sat and ate with his mama and papa and nobody else. He started to feel a little bit bigger and a little better. After supper he asked if he could go down and stay with Claudia and Roy, and Papa said, "All right son, but not too long. It's late."

Matthew went down — past the same people who sat on the stoop most every summer's night, and past Big Jerry, who had been away since spring because he had stolen a car. He stood there, watching Roy and Claudia dance, listening to them talk and laugh. He didn't say much. He just stayed quiet in the cool night, near people who cared about him, till he felt very, very sleepy and went up to bed even before his mama called him.

When Matthew woke the next morning he found that Mama had gone to the store, as she did every Friday, and that today Claudia was staying

home to mind Stevie. She fixed cold cereal for
Matthew, and after breakfast he took his book
and told Claudia that he was going to the new
bookmobile.

Claudia laughed and said, "You gonna find
something in those books of yours that'll do us
any good?" But Matthew just looked away without answering. Claudia rumpled his hair and said,
"You take care, hear?" and Matthew went off to
return his book.

On the corner, one block away from the closed library, Matthew saw the long green bookmobile. He walked up to the truck, climbed the three little steps, and walked inside. A girl who looked a little like Claudia took his book from him. The pretty lady from the library was standing next to her, stamping books for people

to take home. She smiled when she saw Matthew and said, "You look around, dear. I'll come over as soon as I can and help you find a book you'll like."

Matthew smiled back and walked around the bookmobile, looking for the children's section. There were other people walking around too, and they were all close together because there wasn't a lot of room. The books were lined up against the wall on shelves and when you walked behind cubbies and around them you couldn't find a place to be by yourself. Matthew saw that he couldn't stay at the bookmobile the way he could at a real library. So when he came to the children's section he looked through the shelves and tried to find a book as fast as he could. He looked at the titles and all the bright book covers till his eyes fell on a book with a picture of a boy on it. The boy had brown skin just like Matthew's and he looked about the same age. Matthew thought it would be nice to read a book about a boy who looked so much like himself, so he picked it up and took it to the lady, and she said, "You picked out a good book all by yourself." Then she took his card and stamped the book.

Matthew wanted to start his book right away, so he walked straight home. When he got there, Mama was putting groceries away. She hugged him and said, "Hello, sugar," and he hugged her back, took a handful of grapes from the open bag in the sink, and went to his room with his brand-new book.

After he looked at the picture of the boy on the front cover, Matthew turned the book over to look at the back cover. Just then Stevie woke from his nap and began to howl. Mama came in to see what was wrong. She picked up the baby and held him, but he kept howling and howling. She put him on the floor and he took a few steps, but then he fell down and howled some more.

Matthew picked up his book and took it to the bathroom. He locked the door, sat down, and looked at the back cover. There were pictures of some houses on a street that looked like his street. Matthew had never seen a picture like that before, not on the cover of any book he had read, and he was still looking at it when Claudia banged on the door.

"Hey," she yelled. "You staying there all day? Roy's coming pretty soon and I've got to get ready."

Matthew took his book, left the bathroom, and went out the front door. He stood outside for a few minutes, just leaning against the door, and then he climbed the stairs, all the way up to the roof. He pushed open the heavy door and stepped onto the tar-covered floor. Three ladies were hanging clothes on the line and talking, and in a corner two big boys were sitting, playing a radio very loud. The roof was no better for reading and sitting quiet than home was, so Matthew went down again, down all the steps and out to the street.

He went up and down the streets, in and out of alleys, searching for a quiet place. But he found none. His school was across the avenue and down three blocks. He walked by it and wandered around till he came to the park. He

passed mothers with baby carriages, children playing in the playground, big kids playing ball. He crossed a path, and kept going until he saw a high, sloping, grassy hill near the back of the park.

He climbed up to the top, where there was a great big leafy tree with four smaller trees around it. The trunk of the big tree made a chair and Matthew sat on it. When he looked down he saw people walking on the path, but they looked far away, and he could hardly hear them. When he looked up he saw a ceiling of leaves with little patches of sky and sunlight showing through.

He sat there, just watching the breeze move the leaves around, till a stronger chill wind came and made the leaves shudder as the sun hid behind a dark cloud. A shiver ran through him, and though the wind stopped and the sun came out once more, Matthew felt no warmer. It was almost autumn, and after autumn came winter and the snow would cover his tree. Winter would come and where would he go?

Matthew huddled against his tree trunk, holding his book, and then he thought of another boy, the boy in the book he had just finished, the boy who lived way out west, a long, long time ago. He thought how that boy had gone looking for new places and traveled far when the way was hard. Yet the little boy kept looking, even though the winter was bitter cold. The little boy in the West was hungry lots of times and had to find his own food. Matthew felt lucky — it was still summer now, with time to look for a new place and still be warm. And tomorrow

Matthew's mama would give him a great, big, hot breakfast. Tomorrow, right after breakfast, Matthew would go place-hunting. He would find a quiet place and have it all ready for winter. He would start with his own basement, and if that wasn't right, he'd search on. He had found an outside place. He could find an inside one. And then after autumn and winter, spring would come round again and Matthew could come back to his tree.

Matthew rolled over on his tummy and lay flat on the soft grass. He put his book down on the ground with the front cover facing him, and with his finger he traced the picture of the boy. Then he leaned his elbow on the grass, rested his chin in his hand, and opened to page 1.